DEAD MAN WALKING

REVISED EDITION

BOOK 1 –
MISADVENTURES OF THE
CHOLUA BROTHERS

MAGGIE MAGOFFIN

Author Credits: Aspen Lane Photography " Reliving the Past Studio"
Logo Artist – Nan Wright

ISBN: 978-0-9909425-1-1 (sc)
ISBN: 978-0-9909425-2-8 (e)

Because of the dynamic nature of the Internet, any web addresses or links contained in this book may have changed since publication and may no longer be valid. The views expressed in this work are solely those of the author and do not necessarily reflect the views of the publisher, and the publisher hereby disclaims any responsibility for them.

Any people depicted in stock imagery provided by Thinkstock are models, and such images are being used for illustrative purposes only. Certain stock imagery © Thinkstock.

Second Edition – 2/20/2015

All glory be to God! By his mighty power at work within us he can accomplish infinitely more than we could ever dare to ask.-Ephesians 3:20

Tailing Tales of Colorado

The golden yellow piles of debris referred to as *tailings* seen along the mountainsides of Colorado are much more than mere piles of waste rock and dirt. Many hold potential treasure yet undiscovered.

Just as those *tailings* hold such treasures, I hope my stories bring to you a treasure-trove of never before told tales and historical facts you find informative and entertaining.

Maggie M

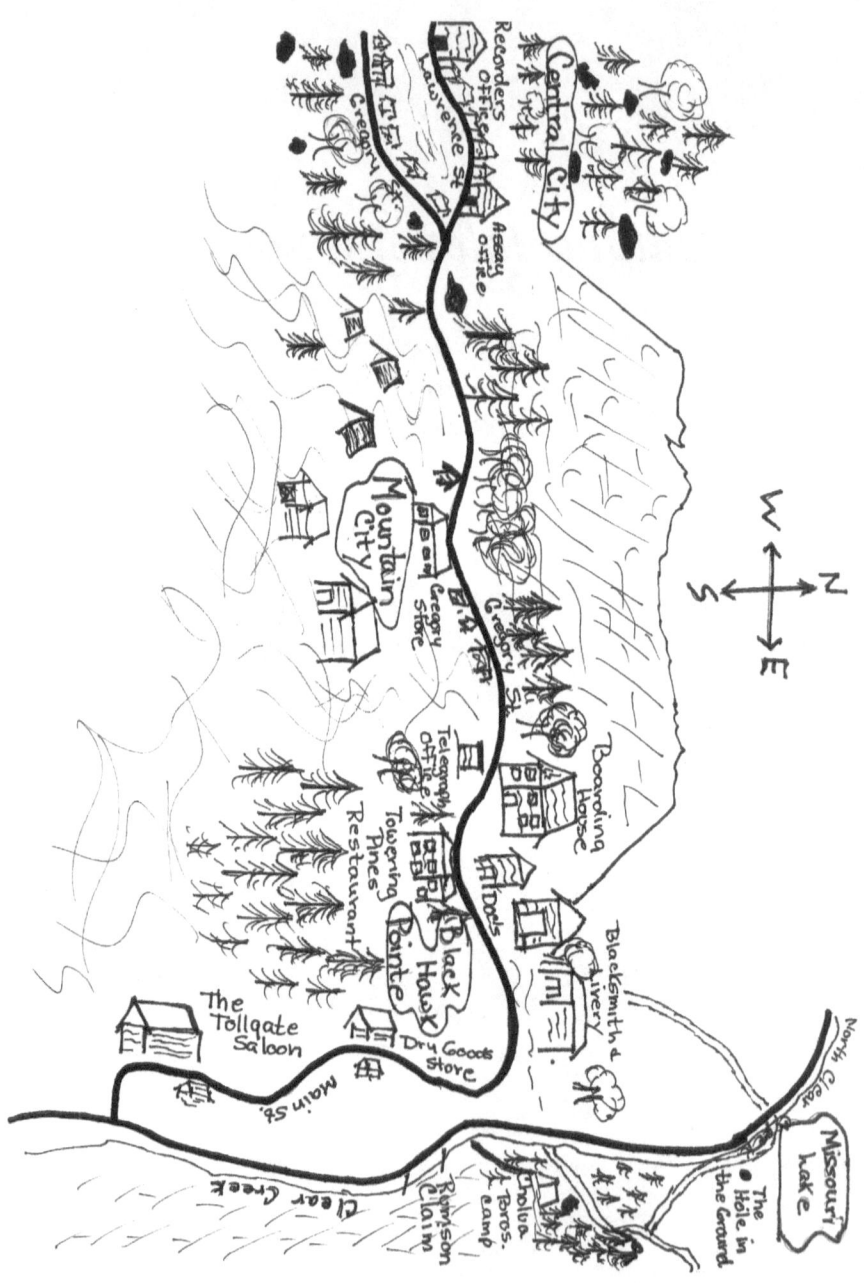

CHAPTER 1

Black Hawk Pointe, Colorado
August 1860

"Is he dead?"

"If he weren't dead, would I be diggin' this hole to bury him?" Dane sighed and looked up at his younger brother, Jake.

Jake hurried away and Dane grumbled as he dug. "Dad-blamed drunk would have to die down here. Oh, no, you couldn't just drop dead in the street. Had to roll down the hill and break your neck. You couldn't end up in the creek and wash downstream where I'd never seen you. Nope, you had to go and die right out in the open." He tossed another shovel-full of the rocky brown earth over his shoulder and then looked at the prone body lying next to him. "Don't even know who you are, feller. Never seen you before but from the whiff I got of parfume and whiskey, I'd say you spent last night at The Tollgate."

With Big John Schmidt at his side, Jake rounded a large boulder along the creek. Each man carried a shovel and they chattered like a couple of females.

1

"What you got there, Dane?" Big John flashed a wide smile. "Jake here says you're buryin' some feller."

Now standing waist high in the hole, Dane didn't miss a thrust with his shovel. "If you two ever stop your yappin' and get down here and help me I'll get er done a mite sooner."

Big John squatted on his haunches, sniffed and poked at the lifeless form lying on the ground. "I'd say he's mighty drunk but I don't think he's dead."

Dane's jaw tightened. "And what makes you an authority on ifin a man is dead or not?"

The muscular blacksmith stood, casting a long shadow over Dane. Rubbing an oversized hand across a furrowed brow above deep-set brown eyes, he shook his head. "I don't know folks as well as I know horses." He pointed at the body lying at his feet. "But I'm tellin' you that man ain't dead."

Just then, the dead man groaned and his right foot twitched. In one smooth movement, Dane jumped from the hole and knelt next to the prone body, the skin around his eyes tightening. The man on the ground was square-shouldered, forty or so. His mustache and hair were black with a hint of gray. He wore a black, tailored suit. Not the sort of man you'd expect to find passed out drunk.

The stranger groaned as he raised himself up on his elbows and then put his right hand across his forehead. "What in tarnation?"

Big John positioned himself behind the stranger and helped him to sit up. "Take it easy there, mister. Looks like you took quite a thump to the back of your head."

The man ran long fingers through a thick, bloody mat of hair and winced. "Where am I?"

Dane leaned on his shovel and sighed. "You're in Black Hawk Pointe. Where'd you come from? And while you're at it, mind tellin' us who you are?"

The man looked around somewhat foggy-eyed and then focused on Dane. "Name's Rumson . . . Ben Rumson."

Jake bent down and helped the man to his feet. "Where you from, Mr. Rumson?"

The stranger brushed dust and debris from his front, still standing a little unsteady. "No need callin' me Mr. Rumson; just call me Ben." The man looked around Jake and then turned and directed his attention to the ground behind Big John. "Any of you feller's seen my hat?" His eyes opened wide and he pointed up the creek bank. "Yup. There it is." He lumbered up the embankment, retrieved a dusty, black top hat and then skidded back down, coming to stand in front of Big John.

The towering man steadied the drunken stranger with one hand. "Woe there mister. You might wanna set a spell 'till you get your legs back."

Dane remained leaning on his shovel. "So where you from and what brings you to Black Hawk Pointe?"

Ben chuckled and then cleared his throat. "You might say I'm from a little bit of everywhere and nowhere in particular."

Dane sighed with disgust and climbed back inside the hole he'd been digging. He scraped a shovel full of dirt back in. "Well, if Big John hadn't shown up, I suppose you'd be callin' Black Hawk Pointe your permanent residence." He looked up at Jake. "How 'bout you get down here and help me fill this in b'for some poor fool stumbles into it."

Jake stepped to the edge of the would-be-grave and narrowed his eyes. "You ain't bein' very neighborly, Dane. Poor Ben here took a good tumble down that creek bank. We probably ought to run him up the hill and get him checked out."

Dane pulled a kerchief from his pocket, removed his weathered, brown felt hat, wiped the sweat from the inside and then plunked it back on his head. Laying the shovel on the ground, he half sat on the edge of the hole and looked up at the three men staring down at him. Studying Ben's face, he decided there was something about the man he didn't like. He seemed weak, but there was also something mysterious there.

He crossed his arms and squinted at the stranger. "Where you stayin', Ben?"

"The Tollgate."

"How long you in town fer?"

Ben folded his arms across his chest and stood his ground. "Long as it takes."

"Takes to what?"

Ben laughed, "Get rich of course!"

Jake and Big John laughed. Dane remained stoic and uncertain. "Get rich, huh? You buy a minin' claim? Plannin' on minin'? Them there hands of yours don't look like they'd fit a shovel. More like—maybe you're plannin' on gettin' rich from other men's labors. That it?"

Ben's lips tightened and his eyes glistened like blue ice. "You callin' me a crook?"

Big John stepped between Dane and Ben. "Okay, fellers, that's enough. He faced Ben and offered his oversized hand. "Ben, we're glad to meet you. This here's Dane and Jake Cholua and I'm John Schmidt. Dane's a mite grumpy today and you'll hafta ignore him. These boys been minin' their claim for near six months now and ain't pulled out enough gold to keep their bellies full, much less put a decent roof over their heads." He smiled at the man in the hole. "Ain't that right Dane?"

Dane nodded and gripped his shovel. "Yeah, I guess." He had to admit the past months of backbreaking work with little to show for it was getting the better of him. "Sorry, Ben. I'm not normally so—unfriendly." He quirked a smile at Big John. "Why don't you take our friend here up the hill to the doc. Jake and me will get this hole filled in and we'll catch up with you later."

Ben reached down and shook Dane's hand. "Thanks for not buryin' me. Sorry we got off to such a bad start. How about you, Jake and John join me for supper tonight at The Tollgate? Meal and drinks are on me." He looked back at Big John. "Won't be necessary to get me checked out. Takes more than a roll down a hill and a thump on the head to take Ben Rumson down."

Big John dropped his arm across Ben's shoulders and the two men rambled off along the creek, disappearing at the bend just beyond the big boulder.

Dane scraped a pile of dirt into the hole and then stood upright, his gaze focused on the ground at his feet. Something glittered, he was certain of it. Something shiny lay beneath the earth. He plunged his shovel into the ground, threw dirt over his shoulder and then dug faster, sending soil scattering in all directions.

Jake stepped out of range of the flying debris. "Have you lost your mind? You were fillin' that hole up and now you're throwin' dirt out. I'm thinkin' the sun's gettin' to you."

Dane grinned and then shouted, "Gold! It's Gold!"

CHAPTER

J ake joined Dane in the hole and the deeper they dug the more gold they found.

About an hour later, Dane stopped digging and looked up at the waning sunlight. "It's gonna be dark soon and Big John and that Rumson feller are gonna be expectin' us at The Tollgate. How's 'bout you go clean up and join 'em? Drop a couple of lanterns off on your way back and I'll keep diggin'."

"You crazy? I ain't gonna' stop now." A smile crossed Jake's dirt-covered face. "Dane, we're rich. Ain't this what we been workin' fer all these months? Nope, I ain't stoppin' to have no dinner. I'll dig till mornin' if I gotta."

Dane lowered his head and then let loose a belly laugh. He laughed so hard he dropped his shovel and doubled over.

"Have you lost yer mind? What in tarnation's come over you?"

Dane pointed up and took a deep breath. "We dug ourselves down here so deep I ain't sure how we're gonna get out."

"You're right. Guess we got ourselves into quite a fix." Jake raised his eyes and shouted, "Help!"

Dane put a large, grimy hand over his brother's mouth. "You crazy? So far it don't appear anyone knows anythin' about this.

I'd kinda like to keep it that way—at least until mornin' when the recorder's office opens and we can stake our claim."

Jake's eyes widened and he pushed back his dirty, black felt hat. "Never thought of that! I been diggin' so hard and my heart's been beatin' so fast since we found this here gold I plumb ain't thought of much else but gettin' rich."

"I know. It's gonna' be hard to keep this quiet, but nobody can know until we get our claim filed." Dane stared into the night sky and then lifted one leg. "Give me a boost."

Jake dropped to all fours and Dane stood on his brother's back, raising him up high enough to climb out. "Almost there. Go up just a little and I think I can make it." He grunted and pulled at the ground above until he could crawl out of the hole. Lying on his back on the cold, damp dirt, Dane caught his breath. "I'll get a couple of lanterns and a ladder and I'll be right back."

From the sounds coming from the hole, Dane could only conclude his brother resumed his digging. "Gold!" He danced a little jig as he walked. "We finally did it!" A full moon lit his path as he made his way to camp and Dane looked toward the ebony heavens and smiled. "Thank you, Lord."

Ten minutes later, Dane was on his way down the hill with two lit lanterns in one hand and a rickety, wooden ladder in the other.

Big John's voice carried on the quiet night air. "Can't imagine where those two could be. They never pass up a free meal."

Ben Rumson replied, "Well, they don't seem to be anywhere around here."

Dane's heartbeat quickened as he picked up his pace, hopeful that Big John and Ben didn't see his lanterns and would head back to The Tollgate.

Reaching the hole where he left Jake, Dane held a shining lantern over the dark abyss. "You still in there?"

His brother's white teeth shone bright in his blackened face. "Wondered when you'd get back. Didn't see Big John and Ben did you?"

Dane's throat tightened as he lowered the ladder into the hole. "Were they here?"

"Nope. But I heard them walkin' by up on the road."

Dane gazed up the hill from where he'd just come. "Let's pull some of those fallen logs over this here hole and head on up to camp. Don't want that there Ben feller knowin' bout this."

Leaving the lanterns and shovels in the pit, Jake scurried up the ladder and they pulled debris over their find.

Dane paced off 25 feet from where they were digging and then began piling rocks. "Help me make a couple more of these."

Wearing an ear-to-ear grin, Jake pushed his dirty, felt hat back from his forehead. "What are you doin'?"

Adrenaline pulsed through Dane like a locomotive but he forced himself to remain calm and think. He heard so many stories from the old prospectors and tried to recall all he learned within a few seconds. "We need to mark our claim before we go to the recorder's office."

With their discovery hidden and marked, the brothers headed up to their campsite. A few yards from their tent, Dane spotted Big John and Ben lumbering down a steep incline toward the road.

Jake called out, "Hey, you lookin' for us?"

Dane groaned and shoved his little brother. "Are you crazy?"

Ben waved his fancy hat and shouted. "There you are." The two men climbed back up the hill and joined Dane and Jake. Ben adjusted his top hat back on his head. "Thought you were gonna join us at The Tollgate. When it got so late, John and I figured we'd best come check on you."

Dane rolled his eyes at his brother and then worked to concoct a believable story as to why they'd taken so long. "Sorry. After you left and we got that hole filled in, some fellers came by lookin' for help to get one of their friends out of a fix." He hesitated as he contrived the tale. "Yeah . . . seems some feller fell down a vertical shaft up there and they was havin' a heck of a time gettin' him out."

Big John frowned. "Who was it? Is he okay?"

Dane had to think fast. Big John knew every miner and would-be miner in the district. "Not sure who the feller was but he's fine. He got banged up a bit. Nothin' serious."

"Where's the shaft?" Big John's eyes widened. "You sure he's okay? Some of them holes go pretty deep."

Dane hated lying to his friend. He'd trust Big John with his life and there was no doubt the man would keep their secret. However, there was Ben Rumson and Dane didn't trust him. Not one bit.

Ben removed his top hat and scratched his head. "You two hungry?"

Jake's stomach growled.

Dane sighed. "Give us a few minutes to clean up and we'll join you up at The Tollgate." He nudged his brother in the direction of their tent and then turned to Big John and Ben. "You two head on up and we'll see you there in 'bout a half hour."

Ben started down the hill, but John stood firm with his arms folded across his chest. "You go on, Ben. I'll catch up with you later." Staring at Dane, he arched an eyebrow. "You gonna tell me what's really goin on?"

Dane shrugged, " Nothin' why?"

"There wasn't no accident, was there?"

Dane watched Ben until he disappeared into the darkness. Then, he slapped John on the shoulder and grinned. "No foolin' you."

"So what's up?"

With a broad smile crossing his face, Jake shoved the big man. "We found gold."

John's eyes widened, "Where?"

Dane slapped his thigh and laughed. "In that hole I was diggin' to bury Ben?"

After several moments of the Cholua brothers recounting their discovery, and John joining in their elation, he scratched his head and shrugged. "Well if that don't beat all."

Dane grew quiet. "Now, you can't tell nobody 'till we get our claimed filed—especially that Rumson feller. Okay?"

John nodded. "Good idea. I'm gonna head on up to The Tollgate, and you two had best get up there before he gets suspicious that somethin's up."

Thirty minutes later, Jake and Dane entered The Tollgate Saloon. Arched windows lined one wall of the massive room, its rough-hewed wooden floor showed signs of weathering and wear. From behind the shiny, mahogany bar, Sam the bartender shouted, "What can I get you, fellers?"

Ben rose from the table in the corner of the room. "Give 'em whatever they want, Sam. Drinks and grub are on me tonight."

Dane slapped his hand on the bar. "I'll have a beer and the biggest steak you got."

Jake stepped his right foot up onto a brass rail at the bottom of the bar. "I'll have the same." He nodded toward a humidor sitting behind the bar. "And give me one of them cigars. I believe Mr. Rumson said anything we like and I'd like a cigar."

Sam was a small, wiry man, quick with a smile beneath his waxed, black handlebar mustache. In his freshly pressed white dress shirt and dark green vest beneath his bartender's apron he gave the impression of a calm, peace loving man everyone called friend. However, Sam was as quick with the Winchester he kept beneath the bar as he was with a smile.

Dane drank a long swallow of his beer and then glanced up at the deer heads mounted on the wall. "Gotcha a new one since I was in here last."

"Guess you ain't been in here in awhile. Joe Casto took that big one down last winter. Took it into Denver and got it mounted but then he didn't have a wall to hang it on. Asked me if I wanted it and—well there it is."

Dane whistled low. "That's one big buck. Biggest rack I've seen in these parts."

Ben called out from across the room. "You two get on over here and join us. Want to thank you proper for taking such good care of me this mornin'."

Big John roared with laughter as Dane and Jake made their way to Ben's table. "It ain't that funny," Dane said through a tight grin.

"Oh, yeah it is," Big John said. "Gotta say, Dane, ain't never in my days before stopped a feller from buryin' a man who weren't dead."

The four men laughed and swapped stories for the next few hours as Dane and Jake enjoyed their steak dinners and drank a few too many beers.

CHAPTER

Dane winced as the drumbeat in his head grew louder. He moaned as the morning sunlight brought a pounding behind his eyes. "Oh, no!" he groaned. "What did we do last night? How much did I drink?"

Jake rolled over on his makeshift cot and faced his brother, with one eye open and a hand to his forehead. "Would somebody please stop that poundin'?"

"I don't even remember how we got back here. Do you?" Dane asked.

"Last thing I remember was dancin' with that pretty gal, the room spinnin' and my head bangin' on the bar room floor."

Dane rose from his cot, pulled back the flap to the tent, and then took two steps backward with his hands over his eyes. "What day is it?"

"You're askin' me? Let's see—yesterday was Monday—I think. So I guess that makes today Tuesday."

Dane gasped as sudden realization hit him. "Hurry up and get dressed. We gotta get to the recorder's office."

In a flash, Jake's feet were in his boots, britches pulled over his long johns and then he plunked his tattered black felt hat on his head. Dane shoved him through the tent opening and they nearly ran as they made their way up the hill toward Central City and the recorder's office.

As they waited in line, Dane fingered a few pieces of gold he pulled from their diggings and watched the clock on the wall. Movement at the front of the line drew his attention to a man in a black top hat talking to the recorder.

"Yes sir, Mr. Roberts! And there's plenty more where that came from. Funniest thing. Yesterday mornin' I found myself passed out at the edge of the creek. I'd had a bit much to drink the night before. As I sat up, somethin' sparkled at the edge of the water. Well sir, there was these pretty nuggets sittin' there just waitin' for me to pick 'em up. After I dug around some, I found a few more and decided I'd best get in here and file a claim before somebody else got to my find."

Dane pushed the men ahead of him aside. Amidst grumblings and threats he made his way to the front of the line and stood looking up at Ben Rumson. Ben smiled, "Well, hey there, Dane. What are you doin' here? You and that brother of yours finally find gold?"

Dane pulled himself up to his full five feet eight inches and seethed, "So you found yourself a claim did you, Ben?"

"Funny thing you know. Right down there along the creek just down from you boys' camp I found these here nuggets." He opened his hand revealing three gold nuggets. "Found 'em yesterday. Not sure how the claim's gonna play out but I panned more this mornin' and it looks like a really good place to start."

Jake stepped up beside Dane. "What's goin' on?"

Dane pulled his pistol from his gun belt and then shoved the barrel into Ben's chest. "Yeah, Mr. Rumson. What's goin' on?"

The building cleared, leaving the recorder, Jake, Dane and Ben alone and a parcel of people peeking through the windows.

Jake laid his hand on Dane's arm. "Whoa there brother! You don't want to do this."

Dane pressed the barrel harder and cocked the gun. "He's jumpin' our claim."

The recorder pulled a Winchester from under the counter. "Put that away, sir. Don't make me call Sheriff Peck over here."

With slow movement, Dane uncocked his pistol, removed it from Ben's chest and then returned it to his holster. "I'm tellin' you, this man is a thief and a liar. Jake and I found that gold yesterday and he had nothin' to do with it." He laid the few nuggets from his pocket on the counter. "If you don't believe me just ask Big John. He was there yesterday mornin'. He knows what happened."

Ben straightened his shirt and jacket and then cleared his throat. "If you're speakin' of John Schmidt, he left early this mornin'. Some feller rode into town with an urgent message for Mr. Schmidt, tellin' him his mother was ailin' in Kansas and he needed to get there as soon as possible."

The recorder interrupted, "Well gentlemen, it looks like we have a problem. Mr. Rumson was here first and he says the claim is his." He looked at Dane. "You sir, say it's your claim." The man lowered the Winchester. "Which of you fellers marked out the claim?"

Dane puffed out his chest. "That would be me. My brother and I marked it proper last night and I even put our names on a piece of paper under one of the rocks."

Ben rolled back on his heels. "Now there sir is the crux of the situation. If you go down to the creek and check out that claim you'll see my name on those pieces of paper and not the Cholua Brothers." He let loose an arrogant laugh. "This man is lying to you, Mr. Roberts. If his name is on those pieces of paper then he is trying to jump my claim."

The recorder rolled his eyes. "Gentlemen, I have no other choice than to record the claim as belonging to the first man here." He pointed a finger at Dane. "If you have a grievance against Mr. Rumson and his claim to this property then I suggest you file that with the Justice of the Peace or the Miner's Association. It is out of my hands."

Dane stormed out of the recorder's office with Jake running to keep up with his brother's quick stride. "What are we gonna do?"

Dane spun on his heel, sweat running down his face and palms cold and clammy. "I'll tell you what we're gonna do. We're gonna find the two fastest horses we can get in this town and we're gonna catch up to Big John. I got me a feelin' his mama ain't ailin' at all." His eyes narrowed and he spat. "No sir. This ain't over by a long shot. Rumson knew exactly what he was doin' when he got us drunk last night and I'd wager he was behind that messenger ridin' into town this mornin'."

The next day, as the sun set and the horizon burned orange and blue, the Cholua brothers caught up to Big John. He'd set up camp at the fork of Clear Creek and Ralston Creek. He was roasting a fresh rabbit on the fire and as Dane and Jake dismounted, the big man greeted them with a smile. "What you fellers doin' here?"

Dane inhaled the aroma of the roasting rabbit and his stomach growled. "Hope you got more than one of them critters. Jake and me are a mite hungry after ridin' like a couple of wild savages trying to catch up to you."

John shouldered his Winchester. "I'll have a couple more directly." Stepping into a thicket of brush a few yards from camp, he stopped and looked back. "I know you didn't track me down just to eat fresh rabbit."

Jake splashed water on his face from the creek and then wiped the moisture away with his shirtsleeve. "You get the rabbits—and after a good night's sleep we're headin' back to Black Hawk Pointe."

John shrugged and then disappeared in a thicket of trees.

Dane squatted next to the creek, splashing cool water on his face and neck. "You think he's gonna believe us—I mean that his ma ain't ailin' and Ben set the whole thing up just to jump our claim."

Jake grinned, "Brother I have every faith you're gonna convince him. Ain't nobody got the gift of persuasion like you." He headed toward the campfire and then stopped and turned around. "You talked me into leavin' Chicago and comin' out to this God forsaken country to find gold. Left a great job, a pretty gal, Ma and Pa to come here." He walked on, "Yep, I'm pretty sure you're gonna convince Big John that Ben Rumson is a thief and a liar."

CHAPTER

4

The sun rose bright and intense as Dane groaned and then stepped from his bedroll. His back ached as he stretched and twisted to work out the kinks from a cold night on the hard ground. Squinting into the irritating sunlight, he kicked at Jake's prone body beneath a worn, blue woolen blanket. "Come on li'l brother let's get movin'"

Jake swatted at Dane's leg and grunted. "I'm comin'".

Dane scanned the campsite and surrounding area. "Where's Big John?"

Looking into the stand of trees where they tied their horses, he saw his friend's buckskin was gone. He kicked at Jake again and then grabbed his saddle as he headed toward the two remaining horses.

Jake rose to his feet, rubbing his eyes and stretching. "What are you in such an all-fire big hurry about?"

Dane tightened the cinch on the black gelding he borrowed from Sam. "Big John's gone! I can't believe he'd just take off like that—without a word."

The sound of hoof beats behind him caused Dane to turn. Big John created a cloud of dust as he reined his charging mount to a quick stop. After hitching his horse to a low hanging tree branch, he looked behind him and then shaded his eyes with his hand as he searched the far-off hillside.

Jake yawned and then grinned. "I'm sure glad you're back. Dane was havin' a conniption. Where'd you go?"

Big John paced back and forth, ducking beneath tree branches, squinting and grunting as he searched the surrounding area. "Shhh!" The big man bent low. "Squat down and keep quiet!" He untied the reins of his horse and handed them to Jake. "Take the horses deeper into the trees. Then get your rifle and get back here."

The hairs on the back of Dane's neck rose as he scanned the hillsides. *Injuns? Bandits? Maybe a mountain lion—or a bear? Nope, Big John would've shot it if it were a critter.* He squatted low and then made his way to his friend's side and whispered, "What is it? What did you see?"

"Not sure, but I'm thinkin' someone's followin' me."

Dane squinted and scanned the open land in front of him. "What do you think they want?"

"Ain't sure but I seen a feller in a dark hat and coat ridin' a sorrel between Black Hawk Pointe and here. I figured we was goin' the same direction and maybe we could ride together. Every time I stopped and waited for him to catch up, he disappeared again. Then, I seen him this mornin' sittin' on his horse on that hill over there." Big John pointed at a rise to the west.

Dane stood, rubbed his legs and then resumed his squat next to Big John. "Well, I don't see him now. Why don't we go back to camp and rustle up some breakfast while I tell you why Jake and I came after you?"

Big John stared across the open land and then stood. "May as well. Don't look like that feller is anywhere around. I'm mighty hungry and I am curious why you rode all this way."

As they neared the campsite, they found Jake squatting close to the ground, his Winchester aimed and at ready. Dane snickered and then winked at Big John, "Watch this."

With slow, silent steps, Dane snuck up behind his brother and then tapped him on the shoulder. Jake jumped. His rifle fired with a loud *Pow!* He turned and faced Dane with a puckered tight mouth and furrowed brow. "That weren't funny, Dane!"

The older brother doubled over laughing as Big John wrapped a beefy arm around the younger brother's neck and chuckled. "Oh, yeah it was!"

The three men relaxed around the campfire as they drank their coffee and ate the remains of the previous night's bounty. Big John ripped a leg piece off his rabbit but before indulging, he pointed it toward Dane. "Now tell me why you followed me."

Dane shared the story about Ben Rumson jumping their claim, reciting with some embellishment the events that took place in the recorder's office. He wiped his mouth with the back of his hand and then took a long swallow of coffee. "That's pretty much what happened. I couldn't figure out how Ben knew about the gold and then it occurred to me that since you'd been with him that whole time after we didn't bury him, you might know how he found out."

John shook his head. "Now that's a mystery. You're pretty much correct about me bein' with him." He puckered his thick lips. "There was about an hour or so when he left me at The Tollgate. He said he needed to go talk to some fellers about business."

Dane arched his eyebrows. "When was that?"

"Not long before we came lookin' for you. When he got back, he said it was gettin' late and he was gettin' hungry. He said we should go up to your camp and see what was keepin' you."

Dane nodded. That had to be about the same time he and Jake were in the hole. "That theivin' crook musta seen us and figured on comin' back after he got us drunk."

Dane tossed the remains of his coffee into the campfire. Movement on the hillside where Big John saw the mysterious man caught his attention. He jutted his chin in that direction and then spoke in low tones. "That the guy you saw earlier?"

Big John stood, directed his gaze toward the rise and nodded. "Yep, that's him."

Dane motioned with his hand for Jake to come closer. "There's a feller over west of here who's been followin' Big John. I think it's about time we had a li'l chat with him." He looked at his friend and winked. "Don't you think?"

Big John nodded. "Yup. How about you and Jake mount up like you're headin' out, circle around behind him and I'll get my horse and head at him. If he tries to run, you can catch him from the other side."

Dane nodded in agreement and then he and Jake mounted and rode off.

CHAPTER

The stranger jerked the head of his sorrel and then turned to ride west as Big John galloped his buckskin toward the man. Dane and Jake sat mounted, ready to block his retreat.

As Big John road up alongside the unknown man, he grabbed the reins from his hands, and pulled the sorrel to a halt. The man twisted in his saddle and his face went white as he stared down the barrel of Dane Cholua's Winchester. "Wouldn't do that if I were you young feller," Dane said with a grin.

The rider couldn't be much older than twelve or thirteen. Big John dismounted and the boy did the same. He held a black felt hat in his trembling hands and looked up to face the enormous man. "Whatcha . . . whatcha gonna do to me?" he stammered.

A calm grin crossed Big John's face as he placed a hand on the boy's shoulder and then gripped until he winced. "I guess that depends."

The boy's eyes grew wide as he worked his jaw." Depends?"

The big man removed his hat with his other hand and swiped at his brow. "It's gettin' mighty hot out here. Can I trust you to ride over to that clump of trees where we can get some shade?"

The boy nodded in a rapid motion. "Yes sir. I . . . I can . . . I can do that."

Moments later, the three men and their young companion sat around Big John's campsite sharing the remaining rabbit and coffee. The boy ate as if he'd not eaten in days.

Big John dropped his arm across the boy's shoulders. "Okay. You got your belly full and you know we ain't got no mind to put a slug through you. So, would you mind tellin' me why you been followin' me?"

Just then, the big man's eyes grew wide and then he yanked the lad to his feet with both hands. "Hey! You're the feller who told me my ma was ailin.'" He shook the boy hard, raised him up and then let him fall in a heap on the ground. "Speak up, boy! You tell me the truth or I'm gonna whip you like you ain't never been whipped!"

Jake offered a hand to the young man and helped him to his feet. "Calm down, Big John. This kid didn't do all of this on his own. Somebody put him up to it and I got a pretty good idea of who." He nodded toward the boy. "Sit down and tell us who you're workin' fer and what's the story."

A tear slipped down the boy's pale face and he swiped it away with a small, dirty hand. "Ifin I tell, I gotta get outta town. Don't know what that Ben feller might do to me or my ma if he finds out I told."

Jake sat next to the lad. "It's okay. We'll take care of you and your ma. You ain't got no worry about that. Just tell us what you know."

The boy inhaled and then exhaled with a loud *woosh*. "Well, you see, my ma and me we've had it pretty hard since pa died last year in that minin' accident. When Mr. Ben said he'd give me five dollars to deliver a message and follow some feller to make certain he kept goin' toward Kansas, I figured weren't nothin' wrong with that. And five dollars is a lot of money."

Big John braced a foot against the log where the boy sat. "What's your name, son?"

"Timmy."

"So Timmy, you didn't think it were a mite peculiar what Mr. Ben was askin' you to do and that he was payin' you five dollars to do it?"

The boy swallowed hard and looked into the big man's face. "No sir."

Big John took off his hat and scratched his head. "Yeah—guess I wouldn't a thought nothin' of it neither when I was your age." He looked at Dane. "Guess we need to get to Black Hawk Pointe and have us a little talk with Ben Rumson."

Beneath the glow of the full moon, the shadowy streets were eerie and quiet as the four riders made their way into town. A cool breeze brushed across Dane's cheek as he stretched in the saddle. To the east, an orange glow broke on the horizon.

They dismounted in front of the livery. Big John took the reins of Dane and Jake's mounts, along with his own, and then threw open the heavy wooden door. He nodded at Timmy. "That your horse?"

The boy handed the blacksmith the reins and then ran his hand through the mane of the sweaty mare. "I wish." His eyes held a faraway look and his shoulders slumped like those of a man many times his age. "Mr. Ben borrowed him from some feller up in Central City."

Big John's eyes narrowed. "I think I recognize her." He nodded at Dane. "Come around later today after you clean up and get a nap. Don't go near Rumson yet."

Dane yawned and stretched. "I'm too tired right now to go lookin' for Rumson, or any other sort of trouble. I need me some sleep." He bent his head, sniffed and then drew back. "And I definitely could use a bath and some clean duds."

Jake's stomach grumbled and he rubbed his belly. "And I could use a good meal."

Timmy stood next to Big John, lips twisting and eyes squinting as though he wanted to say something but he didn't know how. The blacksmith handed off two of the horses to the young man. "How about you help me rub down these critters and then you join me for some breakfast before you head back to your ma?"

The boy grinned and then grabbed the reins and headed into the darkness of the livery. Big John called after him, "You'll find a lantern hangin' on the door frame."

Moments later, the glow of lantern light filled the darkened interior. The blacksmith yawned. "You two go and do whatever it is you need to do. I'll catch up with you this afternoon, once I've had a meal, a bath and a l'il sleep." He headed inside the livery. "Like I said, don't go lookin' for Rumson just yet."

CHAPTER

T hat afternoon, rested, fed and wearing ragged but clean clothes, Dane and Jake headed for the blacksmith's shop. Entering the building, they found Big John bent over and leaning against an old mule, holding the animal's hind foot in his hand. His forge glowed hot and beads of sweat dripped from the man's face and sparkled on his huge forearms. With nails between his teeth, he glanced in Dane and Jake's direction, nodded and then continued on with his work.

The heat of the forge was more than Dane could handle. It was next to impossible to breathe in such a place and he admired his friend for having such stamina. He wiped sweat from his neck with his kerchief and then motioned for Jake to follow him outside.

Standing in front of the livery, Dane punched his clenched left fist into his right hand. "I just want to find Rumson and take him apart."

The blacksmith came out of the building wiping away sweat with a damp rag. "Just calm down, Dane. You're gonna have to pull out some extra patience with this one." He sat on a wooden bench beneath a spreading cottonwood. "If I'm right, that horse Timmy had belongs to J.H. Gregory. I highly doubt Gregory has any notion of what Rumson is up to as far as the horse or stealin' your claim."

Dane kicked a stone with the toe of his boot. "So, you really think someone as important as Gregory is going to care that Ben Rumson stole our claim?

Big John guffawed. "Maybe not, but he's probably lookin' for his horse. And. I'm thinkin' he's got somethin' to do with the Miner's Association. So he might be able to help you get your claim back."

Dane removed his hat and scratched his head. "Yeah. That recorder feller said somethin' about us filin' some kind of grievance with the Miner's Association."

"If he's part of the Association and we can get him in your corner, I'm pretty sure they'll do somethin' 'bout it."

Jake sat next to Big John. "Where do we find this Association?"

The big man leaned back against the tree and pulled his hat down over his eyes. "Give me a few minutes to cool off and change and we'll head up to Mountain City and find Gregory."

The blacksmith went inside to clean up and Dane paced in front of the open door. Jake lay on the ground in the shade of a large maple, his tattered hat covering his face. Nothing much stirred in town. A stray dog lay in the dusty street. He wagged his tail a few times, asking not to be disturbed, and several horses stood at a hitching rail in front of the dry goods store. A cigar glowed in a window in a vacated building across the street.

With Gregory's horse tied to the back of the wagon, Big John, Dane and Jake rode up the hill. As they passed the Gregory Store in Mountain City, John pulled his team to a halt.

A red haired man rushed out of the store toward the wagon. He offered his hand up to Big John. "Hey there, John. What you up to this mornin'?" The man's gaze went to the animal tied to the back of the wagon. "And where'd you find my horse?"

Big John locked the brake on the wagon and passed the reins off to Dane. "That's a good question."

The blacksmith stepped down and then walked to the back of the buckboard where he untied the mare. "Thought she belonged to you."

The owner took the reins from Big John's hand and smoothed the coppery hair on the horse's neck. "I was wonderin' where she'd gotten off to. She does stray now and then but she always comes back. 'Bout a week ago, she didn't come home. I looked everywhere for her but no one had seen her."

Big John nodded with a tight smirk crossing his lips. "You don't say." He winked up at Dane who remained in the wagon. "Mighty interestin' how I came to have your horse. How's about we find a spot of shade and set a spell? We've got quite a story to tell you'."

Sitting beneath a clump of aspen trees, Big John told J.H. Gregory the story about how he came to be in possession of the man's mare and how Ben Rumson stole the Cholua brother's claim. "That 'bout sums it up. That chiseler done stole Dane and Jake's claim and I suppose he stole your horse. I'd say the man at least deserves a whippin' and at best a hangin.'"

Thunder roared in the distance as dark clouds rolled across the sky. A sudden chilling breeze whipped through the grove, causing the aspen leaves to quake and dropping the temperature at least ten degrees. Dane stepped out from under the shelter of the trees and pulled down the brim of his brown felt hat. His gaze directed toward the far off mountain peaks. "Looks like we could be in for a gully washer."

Gregory took quick strides toward the road, pulling up his collar and then straightening the brim on his hat. "Don't know 'bout you boys but I'm gettin' out from under these trees and headin' inside."

Dane sidestepped puddles of water as he hurried to catch up with the man and then joined him inside the Gregory Store.

Shovels, picks, trowels and gold pans hung on the back wall. Several long rows of hastily built shelves held pants, shirts, hats, lamps, candles, empty glass bottles and a variety of dried meats and canned goods. To the west side of the building sat a long roughhewn pine counter, behind which were more shelves holding tins of a variety of sizes and colors.

The room smelled of sweat, cigar smoke and a mixture of foodstuffs.

Gregory stepped behind the counter and moments later set four cups of hot coffee in front of him.

Dane took up one of the cups, sniffed the steaming brown liquid and sipped. "This has to be the best cup of coffee I've had in many a day. Where'd you get it?"

Gregory set a small tin on the counter. "Roast it and grind it myself."

"Yep, that's mighty good coffee. How much?"

"Two bits a tin."

Dane slid the container back across the counter. "That's a little much for my pockets."

Gregory returned the box to the shelf. "Come see me when you strike it rich."

Dane's jaw tightened as he muttered, "Yeah, right. Like that's ever goin' to happen."

Gregory faced Dane with a smug grin. "I can help. I've helped others find gold. I'd be happy to help you—for the right price."

"How much?"

"Two hundred dollars."

Dane laughed. "Mister if I had $200 in my pocket I wouldn't need your help."

Gregory shrugged, stepped around the counter and then leaned his back against the edge. "Anyway, about this here Rumson feller stealin' your claim. Don't know as how I can do much about it. You could file a grievance with the Association;

but without proof you found the gold first, you don't have much to stand on. Seen cases like this before. Just you and your brother actually witnessed your find?"

Dane nodded. "Yep! Didn't want nobody knowin' 'bout it 'till we filed the claim."

"My advice is to steer clear of that feller and go lookin' for another claim." He smirked. "And next time get a witness."

Big John tilted the brim of his wet hat back from his forehead. "So you're sayin' there ain't nothin' these fellers can do to get their claim back?"

Gregory shook his head. "They can try. They can file a grievance and see how far they get with it. Without a witness that they found the gold first—the Association rarely finds in favor of the person makin' the grievance. It's real hard to prove."

Dane picked his hat up from the counter and then looked Gregory straight in the eye. "What you gonna do about your horse? Sounds to me like Rumson took her without your knowin'. Ain't that horse thieven?

Gregory locked eyes with Dane. "Gonna be mighty hard to prove the man stole my horse when she's standin' in my barn. Now ain't it?"

John shook his head. "You ain't filin' no charges against Rumson for stealin' your horse?"

Gregory's jaw tightened as he lowered his gaze. "Got better things to do then go lookin' for him. If Rumson ever crosses my path—I'll take care of him. Ifin I never set eyes on the man— might be for the better."

CHAPTER

When the Cholua brothers and Big John left the Gregory story, the dirt street had turned to mud. Water droplets fell from the eves of buildings. Leaves and small branches littered the ground. The air smelled fresh and clean and the temperature was rising.

Dane took long quick strides down the hill toward Black Hawk Pointe. Jake hurried next to him. Big John called after them, "Hey! Did you forget we came up in the wagon?"

Dane continued walking with his head down, fists clenched and jaw tight. Jake called to their friend, "Looks like we'll be walkin'."

There was nothing they could do about Rumson jumping their claim. Dane's whole body shook as he kicked hard at tumbleweed blocking his path. His determination increased along with his quickening stride. Slipping in the mud and splashing through water-filled open ruts the man uttered not one word. Someway and somehow, he would find gold before October. They had to build a decent cabin and buy enough supplies to last through the fast approaching, long mountain winter.

A woman in a fancy red dress hurried inside the vacant building across from the blacksmith shop. The door slammed shut. A shadow passed by the window. Dane stopped and stared at the storefront.

Jake caught up and stood next to his older brother. "What's up?"

"Not sure. Somethin' strange is goin' on in there."

Back in camp, Dane stretched out on a damp cot and stared at the stained ceiling of the tent they called home. It wouldn't be long before the small tears grew into bigger splits. What would they do if they didn't find gold soon? They only had $5 left from their grubstake. The few small nuggets he found in that hole weren't worth much more than $25, not enough to build a cabin and stock up for winter.

Jake picked up his fishing pole and a bucket. "I'm thinkin' I'll go catch us some dinner. That okay with you?"

"Just get back before dark. Don't feel like trapsin' up to the lake to fetch you. Know how you get when you're fishin'." Dane grabbed the Winchester from under his cot and tossed it to his brother. "And don't go off without this. Never know what you might run into."

Dropping the fishing pole and bucket to the ground with a loud clatter, Jake caught the rifle. "Hey! This thing could go off."

Dane rolled over, turning his back to his brother.

Several hours later Dane awoke and stepped outside. Little light remained beneath the giant conifers surrounding their camp. The sun dropped slowly behind the mountain range to the west. Locusts played their rhythmic tune and the sound of the rushing water in Clear Creek echoed up the canyon.

The fire ring sat cold with no fish frying and Jake was nowhere around. Dane walked out from beneath the trees and gazed up the hill. Seeing no sign of his brother, he climbed atop the rock cropping behind their tent and searched in all directions. "Dag nab it, Jake!"

After checking his pistol and sticking it in his holster, Dane grabbed a worn jacket from a pile of clothes in the corner. He lit a lantern and carried it into the darkness. His stomach growled and his jaw tightened as he followed the path that led up the hill toward Missouri Lake.

About thirty minutes into his scouting trip, faint shouts of "help" came from the east. The moon slipped from behind a cloud giving enough light for Dane to venture from the trail and make his way toward the sound. He stopped walking and listened.

The cries grew louder, and Dane was certain he was heading in the right direction. He shouted, "I'm coming."

The ground grew soft beneath his feet, as he held the lantern high and slowed his pace. "Where are you?"

"That you Dane?"

"Jake?" He stopped and listened. "Where are you?"

"Down here. Watch our step. It's a long fall."

Dane reached the lantern out. A dark circle in the ground about two feet across lay a few yards ahead. "You okay?" He shouted.

"Not sure."

Dane stepped forward with cautious steps. Reaching the edge of the opening, he held the lantern above the hole. "How in tarnation did you get down there?"

Jake's voice echoed from the abyss. "I'm not sure. I was walkin' along when all of a sudden I took a step and next thing I knew I was lyin' in a heap in the bottom of this hole."

Dane set the lantern on the ground and lay on his belly, sticking his head in the opening. Seeing nothing in the dank darkness, he reached back for the lantern and lowered it in front of him. There on a ledge about fifteen feet down, his younger brother sat with one leg stretched out before him and the other bent at the knee and pulled up against him. "Anythin' broken?"

"Don't think so, but my ankle hurts somethin' awful. Did you bring a rope?"

The older brother shook his head in frustration. "Now why would I bring a rope?" He searched the ground around him and his hand closed around Jake's fishing pole. "Don't suppose this will do much good getttin' you outta there but at least I can lower the lantern down to you and go for help."

Tying the lamp to the end of the fishing line, Dane lowered the glowing light down to his brother. Jake caught hold of the lantern. "Could you bring back somethin' to eat? I'm mighty hungry."

Dane rolled to his back and sighed before standing. Then he squatted next to the hole and called down, "Where's the gun?"

"It fell down the hole with me. Landed right here next to me. You want it?"

Dane's jaw relaxed and his lips formed a slight grin. "No brother. Just keep it 'till we get you outta there."

An hour later, Dane and Big John arrived back at the hole. Dane stuck his head in the opening. The oil lamp still glowed bright on the ledge next to Jake and from the snoring echoing in the pit, it was obvious his brother had fallen asleep. He looked up at Big John. "Think you can lower me down there and then pull us both back up?

His friend held a lantern above his head and looked around. "If we got enough rope to tie off on that tree over yonder, I'm thinkin' so."

With the rope tied to the tree at one end and the other tied to Dane's waist, Big John lowered him down to the ledge.

Dane untied the knot at his waist, squatted next to Jake and then poked him in the arm. Jake's eyes opened wide and he snorted. He blinked as he focused on Dane and then tried to stand. "Where you been?" As he put weight on his left ankle, he winced. "Darn! That hurts!"

Dane reached out to help his brother. "Steady there. We're gonna get you outta here."

Big John's face floated in the lamplight. "You ready to come up?"

"Give us a minute," Dane shouted back.

Setting the lantern closer to the rim of the ledge, he tied the rope around Jake. The glow from the oil lamp reflected off something glittering in the darkness below. He picked up the light and held it out over the dark abyss beneath them. Then he dropped down to lie on his belly and held the lantern out as far as his arm could reach. Not more than ten feet down ran an underground stream littered with something shiny. He inhaled several deep breaths and then held the lantern lower, revealing a large vein of quartz on the opposite wall.

CHAPTER

After a great deal of grunting and tugging, Big John extricated Jake and then shouted down to Dane, "Your turn."

With only the light of the lantern to guide his way, Dane had climbed the rock face beneath the ledge to the ground below. He called back to his friend, "Can you make that hole bigger. The sun should be up soon and I could use more light down here."

"Get outta the way," Big John hollered.

Dane backed into a crevice in the wall and held his arms over his head.

Moments later, rock and dirt fell from above and continued for some time before the blacksmith shouted, "How's that?"

"Great!"

"You comin' up?"

"I'll give you a shout when I'm ready."

"Whatcha doin'?"

"Found some interestin' rock down here and I wanna check it out."

Dane cupped his hands, drank from the stream and then splashed his face. He then held the lantern up and with his other hand he picked something out of the water that looked to be a gold nugget.

At that very moment, the morning sun cast long beams through the opening in the ground, revealing the underground stream with its narrow, sandy banks winding between sheer rock walls. The cavern stretched into blackness at either end and the water at Dane's feet glistened beneath cascading beams of light.

Jake called to his older brother, "Did you bring me somethin' to eat?"

Dane sighed and then hollered back, "It's in that bag up there. You're dang lucky we didn't eat it ourselves. I ain't et since lunch yesterday and I ain't too sure Big John's had anythin' either."

Returning his attention to the stream and its suspected treasure, he picked up several small, shiny pieces, held them in the light and then smiled. "Gold." The word came out just above a whisper. Moving a large rock to one side, he found several more pieces. "Gold!" This time he shouted. "It's gold!"

He pocketed the nuggets, climbed up the jagged rock to the ledge and then tied the rope around his waist. "Pull me up fellers. I'm thinkin' we got us a claim to file."

That afternoon, the three men entered the recorder's office. Jake sat on a bench next to the door with his leg propped up in front of him. He had moaned and groaned all the way down the hill but he still had a smile on his face. "What we gonna call it?"

Dane leaned on the counter waiting for the recorder to prepare the paperwork. "Call what?"

"Our claim. We gotta call it something. It's gotta have a name."

The older brother rubbed his chin and arched his eyebrows. "Since we wouldn't a found the gold if you hadn't fell in the hole, I'm thinkin' you should name it."

Big John guffawed. "I agree with Dane. Seems to me it's only right."

Jake grimaced and then rubbed his leg. "The hole in the ground."

Dane nodded. "Yeah, you fell in a hole in the ground, so what you gonna name it?"

"That's what I wanna call it. The Hole in the Ground."

CHAPTER

9

Dane helped Jake up the stairs at the boarding house. "I could make it up the hill," Jake grumbled.

"You heard the doc. You gotta stay off that ankle for a couple days."

Dane pushed the door to his brother's room open and helped him to a chair. "You couldn't make it up those stairs by yourself and Big John half carried you down the hill."

Jake grumbled something undistinguishable.

With its double bed, a washstand with a white bowl and pitcher, a table and three chairs, one of which was a rocker, the room was much nicer than most.

Dane stood in the open doorway. "Miss Maggie was nice enough to be willin' to take care of you for our last five dollars. I'll come getcha in a couple days. Stay off that foot and stay outta trouble."

"I'm hungry."

"She'll bring your supper up in a little while. You'll probably eat better than you have since we left Chicago, so be nice."

A few hours later, in front of the livery, Dane and Big John finished loading two mules with their equipment and foodstuffs. The blacksmith gave Timmy last minute instructions about running the livery while he was away. "And remember, Timmy, you don't tell no one where we went or what we're doin'."

The young boy grinned wide. "No problem, sir. I'm much appreciative that you trust me here on my own."

The blacksmith ruffled the boy's blond hair. "You been doin' a mighty fine job helpin' out 'round here. I don't think you'll have any problems. If you're not certain about somethin' or need help with anythin', Sam up at The Tollgate can help you out. I told him I was goin' fishin'. That's what you tell anyone who asks."

Timmy nodded. "Yes, sir."

Dane led the mules and Big John carried several canvas bags as they headed to the back of the livery. Rounding the corner of the blacksmith's shop, Dane looked back toward the empty building across the street. Nothing moved inside but he had an uneasy feeling about the place. Shaking off the foreboding, he forced a smile as the sun sank low in the west. "I'd like to get up there before it gets dark." He led the way down a hill to an overgrown path. "I know this is the long way around but I'd rather no one saw us headin' out."

Big John nodded. "Probably a good idea." He chuckled. "Don't recall the last time I went fishin' and took two mules worth of gear."

Reaching The Hole in the Ground just after dark, the men set up camp. Under the light of several lanterns, they built a ladder long enough to reach the ledge where Jake had landed.

As they finished for the night and bedded down beneath a cloudless sky, the beauty of the starlit heavens, the smell of the campfire, and the sounds of breezes wafting through the pines overcame Dane. "Thank you, Lord."

Pulling his hat over his eyes, he was dozing off when the sound of a twig snapping awakened him. Dane listened intently.

Nothing moved. All was quiet. He lay awake for a time and then drifted into a fitful sleep, waking just before dawn.

Rolling up his bedroll and then unpacking what he needed to fix breakfast, Dane then gathered a pile of twigs and several large pieces of wood and restarted the fire. He filled the metal pot with water, tossed in some coffee and set it on the grate above the flames.

"I'll have a cup of that when it's ready." The blacksmith's groggy voice startled Dane from his thoughts.

"Yeah, sure."

"What's up with you?"

"Whatcha mean?"

"You been jumpy as a frog on a hot rock ever since we left Black Hawk Pointe. You hardly said a dozen words on the climb up here."

"You'll think I'm crazy."

Big John sat on a log facing Dane. "No I won't. Promise." He crossed his heart with two fingers.

"I've just got a strange feelin' about that buildin' across the street from the livery."

"The empty one?"

Dane nodded. "Yesterday mornin' before we headed up to see Gregory, I saw what looked like the glow of a cigar from the window." He checked the coffee. "When we got back down the hill, a woman in a red dress hurried inside. Don't know why it's getting' to me. Just somethin' about it don't seem right."

"Nobody's been in there for months."

"That's what I thought."

Big John rubbed the stubble on his chin and shrugged. "Don't know. Like I say, the place is empty."

CHAPTER

10

Jake stared out the window to the street below. Even with his foot elevated on a chair, his ankle throbbed with pain. Three days had passed since Dane and Big John left for The Hole in the Ground. The *plop plop* of raindrops against the pane of glass only amplified his frustration.

A sharp rap at his door startled him from his musings. "Mr. Cholua? I have your dinner. May I come in?"

Just as Dane had promised, Miss Maggie kept Jake well fed and checked on him regularly. Lowering his raised foot to the floor, he then limped across the room. "I'm comin'."

The door swung open. "Mr. Cholua! What are you doing on that ankle? You're supposed to be resting and keeping it elevated. You'll never get better if you don't do what the doc tells you."

Miss Maggie was a statuesque woman with silver grey hair and a ruddy complexion. Though she was congenial and welcoming, her flashing green eyes and no-nonsense tone commanded obedience. With raised brows, she pointed at Jake. "You sit yourself down on that chair and prop that foot up. I'll set your dinner here on the table next to you."

With a sigh of resignation, Jake returned to his chair and did as ordered. "I'm gettin' a mite tired of sittin' here day after day lookin' out that window a watchin' the world go by."

Miss Maggie sat on the edge of the bed. "Maybe I can help get you downstairs tomorrow and you can sit outside."

Jake stood, wincing as he put weight on the injured ankle. "I'm thinkin' I could probably make it down those stairs on my own. It's gettin' better."

"Right. Maybe you could even win a foot race against ole Granny Johnson." She stood in the doorway and smiled back at him. "Eat your dinner and I'll be up later to check on you. And if you're real good, I might even let you lose another game of Faro to me."

The meal was delicious but Jake had little appetite. With his plate on his lap, he lifted a spoonful of taters and gravy to his lips as movement across the street caught his attention. The rain had stopped and the sky cleared allowing the last vestiges of sunlight of the day to peek through. A man in a top hat and black coat stood talking to a woman in a fancy, red dress. Jake was certain the man was Ben Rumson. Setting his dinner plate on the table, he stood and opened the window. "Rumson!" he shouted.

The man turned. Sure enough, it was Ben Rumson. Jake lunged through the window, half in and half out. "Rumson, I want to talk to you! Get up here!"

The man smiled a half-grin, waved his fancy hat and then hurried around the corner of the telegraph office.

Jake's ankle throbbed with pain and he cracked the back of his head on the window frame. Pulling himself back inside, he huffed as he returned to his chair. Rubbing the bump rising on the back of his head, he muttered, "Darn it, Dane. When are you gettin' back here?"

Just then, the door opened and the older brother entered. "What's all the commotion about? I thought I told you to behave yourself." He chuckled and then tossed his hat and a canvas bag on the bed. "Who you yellin' at?"

Jake resisted the urge to lunge at Dane. "Bout time you got back? I'm goin' crazy sittin' up in this room with nothin' to do but eat, sleep and play an occasional game of Faro with Miss Maggie." He pointed out the open window. "And I was yellin' at that no good Rumson feller."

Dane's smile faded as he stepped to the window and peered down. "Where?"

"He ran around the telegraph building when I yelled at him—but not before he gave me a stupid smile and tipped his hat." Jake shook with anger. "What are we gonna do about him? We can't just let him get away with stealin' our claim!"

Dane picked the canvas bag up from the bed, pulled out a small pouch and then crossed the room and spilled the contents on the table. At least a dozen small gold nuggets sparkled in the waning sunlight that shone through the window. "And there's plenty more where that came from." He ran his palm across the treasure and his eyes glowed with an inner light. "I'm thinkin' Gregory might be right. Maybe we need to just forget about Rumson and move on."

Jake rubbed his hand over his lips and then his chin. "I don't know. It just . . . well it just ain't right . . . what he did and all." He reached across the table and palmed several nuggets. His mouth went dry and his pulse quickened as he fingered the treasure. "You got this from The Hole in the Ground?"

"Yep, and Big John has half of what we found."

Jake licked his lips and then poured himself a glass of water. "We're rich?"

"Well, we have enough to build us a cabin and get us through the winter." Dane leaned in closer and sucked in a quick breath. "Since I spent all our money to buy what we needed up at the claim and set you up here, it's a darn good thing."

The younger brother limped across the room and plopped his weather-beaten hat on his head. "Then get me outta here."

"You thinkin' you can make it to The Hole in the Ground? It's a mighty long climb."

"I'm thinkin' first we find Rumson and get him to admit he stole our claim and then we head up there."

Dane shook his head. "Brother, we got our claim and there's no tellin' if we'd of found more gold along the creek." Gathering up the nuggets and then repacking them in his bag, he slung it over his shoulder. "Let sleeping dogs lie."

Jake held tight to the handrail as pain shot through his leg with every step down the stairs. "I ain't leavin' this be, Dane."

"Fine! You get down these steps without breakin' your neck and I'll go look for Rumson. Then I'll bring him back here and you can have at him."

Breathless and worn, Jake reached the bottom of the staircase before replying. He inhaled a deep breath and cringed with the pain radiating up his leg. He rasped, "I'm goin' with you."

Dane sighed. "Big John's up at The Tollgate gettin' a steak dinner. Which is where I planned to take you iffin I thought you could walk that far. From the way you're groanin' and limpin' I'm thinkin' you still shouldn't be on that ankle."

Jake dropped into a chair in Miss Maggie's living room. His head throbbed from the banging it took earlier and the pain in his ankle made him want to scream. Determined to find Rumson, through gritted teeth he told Dane, "Find the doc. Get me somethin' for this pain. Then get me a horse. Rumson's some place in this town and I intend to find that thieven claim jumper."

Dane stepped toward the front door. "I'll go find the doc and get you somethin' for your pain. Then I'll find you a horse. But we ain't gonna run all over town lookin' for Rumson anymore tonight."

"You go have your steak dinner with Big John." Jake crossed his arms in front of his chest. "I'll find Rumson on my own— and I can take care of him myself."

Dane muttered something as he left and then slammed the door shut behind him.

CHAPTER

11

J ake dismounted in front of The Tollgate and then followed Dane into the saloon. Sam greeted them from behind the bar, "Hey, fellers." He shouted over the din of laughter and frolicking, "Get on over here." He waved a hand motioning for them to come closer.

Jake did his best to keep up as Dane forged ahead through a group of miners. In spite of taking the painkiller his brother got from the doc, Jake's throbbing ankle continued to slow his pace.

Standing before the bar, Jake leaned in to speak in Sam's ear, "You seen Rumson?"

Sam shook his head. "Ain't seen him since last night. Mighty strange, too. He's been in here every evenin' since he got to town. Took a room upstairs and been takin' most of his meals here."

Dane pushed in closer to the other two men. "You seen John Schmidt?"

Sam pointed toward the far end of the room. "Yep, down there at the table in the corner." He winked. "Guess you boys found somethin' more than a few trout on that fishin' trip." He pushed at Dane's shoulder. "John got him the biggest steak I had and took a room for the night—paid for it with gold nuggets."

Dane shook his head, sighed and then made his way to John's table, clearing a path through the crowd for Jake to hobble through.

Big John greeted them with smacks on the back and then pulled out the chair to his right. He nodded at Jake. "Have a seat. Not many of 'em around tonight. Don't think I've ever seen this place with so many folks. Heard there's a lady gambler in town and she's runnin' the table in the back room. 'Tween her and the girls upstairs, seems to be a popular place."

Dane grabbed a chair and sat on John's other side.

Jake shouted, "You seen Rumson?"

John's eyebrows arched and he narrowed his gaze on Jake. "What you want with him? Best you take Gregory's advice and leave him be." He pushed back from the table and rubbed his stomach. "We got The Hole in the Ground." He shoved Jake, nearly toppling him out of his chair. "Get a good meal and a full night's sleep and in the mornin' we'll head back up."

The noise in the room dropped from the previous din of laughter and shouting to a low rumble as heads turned toward a short, round man standing in the doorway. Jake recognized him as the clerk from the dry goods store. From the paler of his skin and the trembling of his hands, it was obvious he was not the bearer of good news. His voice cracked. "Got a feller out here on my wagon shot through the head. I was wonderin' if anyone could tell me who he might be."

"Where'd you find him?" A deep baritone voice asked.

The store clerk fingered the brim of his black bowler. "Down along the creek. My boys helped me load him into the wagon."

"You sure he's dead?" Someone else asked.

The man nodded. "No doubt 'bout that. Bullet went clean through the back of his head and come out the front."

Sam came around the bar and then raised his hands in the air. "You folks go back to doin' whatever you was doin' and I'll go check it out. I know 'bout every man in this town. If he's from 'round here, I'll know him."

Moments later, Sam returned and pushed his way through the rollicking crowd to Big John's table. "I'm thinkin' you boys ought to come out front. You ain't gonna believe who's on that feller's wagon."

The store clerk pulled back one end of a canvas cover, revealing the grisly remains of a man's face. "Sam says you know this feller. Says his name's Ben Rumson."

Jake's stomach twisted at the grotesque site before him. He wanted Rumson to pay for stealing their claim. However, killing the man was something neither he nor his brother could have done. He looked at Dane and then at Big John, both standing in mute silence.

The store clerk pulled the cover back over Ben's face and then climbed in his wagon. "I'll leave him at the undertakers and tell him his name. You know if he's from around these parts or got any family?"

Big John shook his head. "Naw—didn't ever say where he was from. Only thing we know about him is he liked his whiskey, he stole John Gregory's horse and he jumped these boys' claim."

Dane nodded. "Yep, that's 'bout it." He rubbed his chin. "Come to think of it, we don't even know for sure Ben Rumson was his real name."

The man on the wagon looked down at the blacksmith. "Sounds like quite a character. You say he stole John Gregory's horse?"

Jake shook off the numbness that overcame him at the site of Ben Rumson lying dead. "Yeah—and he stole our claim."

The store clerk flipped the reins to his team and he smirked. "Could be quite a few folks wantin' this feller dead."

As the wagon rattled down the road, Big John turned to go back inside. "You boys comin'?"

With his head down, Dane shuffled his boot through the dirt. "You go on. We'll be in later."

The wagon disappeared in the darkness as the remains of Jake's lunch coursed up his throat. Limping to the edge of the building he wretched. He'd never before seen anything so gruesome as the mutilated face of Ben Rumson. He wiped his mouth with his shirtsleeve as he returned to his brother, who now sat on a step in front of the hotel. "Whatcha think?" Jake said.

Dane shrugged and then raised his eyes to meet his brother's. "Guess we don't need to go lookin' for Rumson."

CHAPTER

T he raucous crowd had thinned, leaving only a half dozen
miners at the bar and several sitting at tables drinking and
playing cards.

Seeing no sign of Big John, Jake concluded the blacksmith
had gone upstairs. He returned to the chair he had occupied
before the store clerk arrived and then raised his foot to rest it
on the chair next to him.

Dane sat at a chair across the table. He rubbed his forehead
and then raised an eyebrow. "Can't believe he's dead—think it
was the Bummers?"

Jake had been thinking the same thing. "Shot through the
head . . . and from the back. Could be."

With an unsteady hand, Dane picked up his beer and then
drank the glass dry. "Like the feller said, probably a lot of folks
wanted him dead." He stood. "I need another drink."

Jake had heard rumors that several members of the Bummers
Gang had made their way up to Black Hawk from Denver after
the Turkey War, but as far as he knew, he'd not ran into any of
them. He popped a pain pill in his mouth and then swallowed
a long gulp of beer. As he returned his glass to the table, the
door to the backroom swung open. A petite young woman stood

in the doorway. Several men sat at a round table in the smoke-filled room behind her. It was obvious from their grumblings and the scraping of chairs that they were not happy. "Thank you, gentlemen." The woman raised an eyebrow and smiled as she tightened the strings on her reticule. "Pleasure doin' business with you."

The barroom fell silent. Her shiny, red dress that showed off her slim waist and bountiful breast shimmered in the gaslights and swished as she crossed the room. Golden curls fell across her white shoulders as she smiled and nodded at each man she passed.

An overly ardent admirer grabbed her by the arm and she jerked from his grasp. "Shame on you, sir!" With open palm, she pushed the man in his chest and then giggled and shook a finger as he stumbled back and fell over a chair.

Standing at the bar, she smacked her hand on the counter and told Sam, "Your best bottle of whiskey and a cigar, barkeep."

The woman possessed an appearance of sweet innocence. However, John did mention a lady gambler in the back room and she left there only moments earlier. Loud and brash, she knew her whiskey and cigars. Jake assumed the lady bought the drink and tobacco for a gentleman.

Dane stood at the bar wide-eyed and slack jawed. The woman patted him on the cheek. "Better close that up, sweetie, before a bug flies in."

She scanned the room and then to Jake's amazement she walked directly to his table and sat in a chair facing him. She dumped his beer on the floor, half-filled the container with whiskey and then filled her own glass. "I hate to drink alone." Her eyes were brilliant blue and she smelled of lavender and cigar smoke. A curious combination that was somewhat sensual. "She reached her small white hand across the table. "My name's Ruby."

"Jaaa—Jake. My friends call me Jake." His thoughts swirled incoherent as he took her hand in his. "Yeah—Jake—pleased to meet you—Ruby."

The sound of the chair next to him scraping across the floor caused him to bump his glass and splash whiskey on the table. Dane had returned and he stared at the mysterious woman. He had gone to the bar for another beer but he came back empty handed. He jerked his head upward and locked eyes with Jake. "I'm thinking we best be headin' out soon."

Jake picked up his glass, tipped a drink of the burning, sweet liquid and then swallowed hard. "Thank you for the drink, Ruby."

"You're quite welcome, Jake." With her cigar between her lips, Ruby pulled a matchbox from her reticule. She struck a match on the tabletop, held up the flame and then inhaled. Then she sighed. "Now, that is one fine cigar." She blew a smoke ring, her dark-lashed eyes following the trail upward. Then, her attention went to Dane and she reached out her hand. "I don't think we've been introduced. I'm Ruby Cashman."

Dane tipped his hat. "Dane Cholua."

"Thought you was gettin' another drink," Jake said.

Dane's eyes narrowed. "I'm thinkin' one of us needs to keep his wits about him." His gaze went to the bar and then scanned the room. "What with a killer on the loose and all, we can't be too careful."

Ruby held her hand to her breast. "A killer? Here in Black Hawk Pointe?"

Jake swallowed a drink of whiskey. "Now don't you worry your pretty little head about that, Miss Ruby. You're safe with the Cholua brothers. Ain't that right, Dane."

Dane grunted, stood as if to leave and then sat back down. "Wait a minute—the cigar—the red dress. Were you in the empty building across from the livery?"

Ruby inhaled a drag from her cigar. "Maybe—why do you ask?"

Dane leaned across the table coming face to face with the woman. "I seen a lady go in there a few days ago, and that mornin' I saw what looked like a cigar ash glowing in the window."

Ruby let loose a gruff chuckle. "Since when is it a crime for a lady to check out prospective real estate property—or smoke a cigar?" She ran her dainty finger around the rim of her glass. "And you changed the subject. Who got killed?"

Jake held up his glass. "Ben Rumson." He held one finger to the back of his head, mimicking shooting a gun. "Got shot straight through."

Ruby's eyes opened wide. "Ben Rumson shot dead?"

Dane leaned his head to one side. "Sounds like you might of known the man."

She smacked her hand on the table and her face flushed red. "That chiseling good for nothing cheated me out of $200 in Wichita a couple of months back. Rumor was he struck it rich in Black Hawk Pointe." She shook her head. "I can't believe it. I came all the way here to catch up with him and now he's dead."

Dane worked his jaw. "How long you been here?"

The young woman appraised Dane and then met his eyes with hers. "I arrived on the stage last week."

Jake's pulse quickened and his palms sweat every time he looked at the lady. His thoughts spun as he tried to comprehend the complexities of a woman with such a boisterous demeanor and beauty. From the moment she entered the room, he was certain he had seen her somewhere before. Then he remembered seeing Rumson talking to a woman in a red dress in front of the telegraph office. "Was that you I saw talkin' to Rumson across from Miss Maggie's this afternoon?"

Ruby puffed on her cigar. "He said he didn't have it on him but he'd meet me here tonight." She chuckled. "Guess he got a little—detained."

She and Jake laughed but Dane sat stoic. A few moments later, he stood and clasped his younger brother on the shoulder. "I'm thinkin' it's gettin' late and if we're headin' up the hill in the mornin' we'd best be gettin' to bed." His grip tightened. "Don't you think li'l brother?"

"Ouch!" Jake pulled away from Danes grasp. "You go on." He smiled at Ruby. "I'm thinkin' Ruby and I could sit here a spell and get to know one another better." He poured another drink. "Besides . . ." He winked at Ruby. "I'm thinkin' it would be downright rude to leave this pretty lady drinkin' all alone."

Ruby laid her hand on Jake's and giggled. "And it wouldn't be wise for a helpless woman to be all alone with a killer on the loose." She gave Dane an icy stare. "Now, would it, Jake?"

Dane stepped a pace away and then turned and faced Jake. "I'm goin' over to Miss Maggie's and see if we can get a room for tonight." With a tightened jaw, he glared at his brother. "Then I'm comin' back here to get you and you will go with me."

Dane hurried out the door and Jake returned his attention to Ruby. "Guess we got a li'l while to get better acquainted. I gotta ask, Miss Ruby. When can I see you again and how long you gonna be in Black Hawk Pointe?"

CHAPTER

With Dane and Big John leading the pack mules, Jake did his best to keep up. The cool morning air caused him to shudder as he limped along the rocky path with a walking stick.

Last night, he sat across the table from the most beautiful woman he'd ever seen. He might have been sharing breakfast or coffee with the lady at this very moment but once again, much against Jake's desires, Dane managed to change his plans. "I don't see why you're in such an all fire big hurry to get back up there."

Dane turned scowling eyes at his brother. "If I didn't get you out of Black Hawk Pointe, you sure as shootin' would a gone blabin' to that Ruby woman about our claim." He shook his head. "I swear, brother, when it comes to women you ain't got the sense God gave you."

Jake swore beneath his breath and then swallowed a pill followed by a long drink of water from his canteen. From the itching in his boot, he knew his ankle was healing but occasional shots of hot pain still traveled up his leg. Dane and Big John had built a comfortable camp and even the ragged old tent was a welcoming sight after the climb up the side of the mountain.

Dane pegged out his mule and then unloaded gear and supplies. "Don't think you ought to try going down the ladder just yet with that ankle."

Jake knelt on the cool, moist ground at the edge of the large hole and peered into the darkness. "Think there's much more down there?"

Big John finished hauling the last load of supplies from his mule into the tent and then joined Jake and Dane. "That water goes a long ways in both directions. So far, we've only worked about a hundred feet." The big man winked and grinned. "I'm thinkin' since we found as much as we have in that part of the stream, there's gotta be more."

Dane pulled a ladder from beneath a pile of pine branches, carried it to the hole and slipped it over the edge. "And, it looks like there's at least one good vein runnin' down a wall." He descended the first five steps of the ladder. "We've picked at it some but we're gonna need to do some blastin' and start diggin' a shaft before we'll know for certain."

Moments after Dane reached the bottom and lit several lanterns, Big John descended the ladder. Jake lay on the ground, leaning his head and shoulders further into the hole. The light from the lamps perched on the ledge revealed another ladder reaching down to the bank of the underground stream. In the water sat a sluice box and along the edges lay piles of rock and gravel.

"I'm thinkin' I could make it down there if I rest my ankle for awhile." Jake's voice echoed in the cavern. "About the blastin' . . ."

As soon as they reached the bottom of the hole, Big John and Dane began digging from the stream and tossing the wet dirt and rock into the sluice box. Jake sighed with frustration and then lay on his back on the ground next to the opening.

Several hours later, the noises coming from below sounded further away. Jake peered into the hole. Seeing no sign of his brother nor their friend, he called down, "Dane? Big John?" He paused to listen. "You two okay down there?"

Jake rubbed his ankle, took another pain pill and then made his way down the ladders to the edge of the stream. Faint sounds drifted from the darkness to his right. Sunlight streaming in from above lit the area directly below but the lanterns that had set on the ledge were gone. Jake walked along the stream until the bank ended and then stepped into the cold water where the creek turned to the left. Pressing his hands against rock walls on either side and with uncertain steps, Jake followed the waterway. In pitch blackness he called out, "Dane? Big John?"

"That you, Jake?" Dane called back.

"Yeah, where are you?"

The glow of a lantern shone ahead about ten feet and then the older brother appeared. "How'd you get down here?"

Jake huffed. "How do you think? Same way you did."

"Well, you're here now, might as well put you to work." A broad smile crossed his face. "We was right." He held the lantern up higher and showed his palm holding two large, shiny gold nuggets. "There's more of it further upstream."

Jake's heartbeat quickened as he took the nuggets in his hand. He fingered them and then held one closer to the light. "Guess we won't be needin' to do no blastin' then, huh?"

Dane shook his head. "Nope! I'm goin' down the hill in the mornin' and get us some black powder."

CHAPTER

14

D ane took one of the mules and made his way down the mountain to Black Hawk Pointe. After checking on Timmy at the livery and confirming all was well, he headed up to Mountain City and the Gregory Store.

As he stood at the counter waiting for the clerk to return with his order, a tall, slender woman entered. She wore a simple gray skirt, fitted dark blue jacket and black riding hat. With her dark hair, fair skin and dark eyes, she was just the sort of beauty Dane admired but seldom saw, especially since coming west. She nodded and smiled as she passed and then headed to the back wall of the store where she removed a shovel and gold pan.

The clerk returned with a wooden barrel and handed Dane a roll of fuse wire. "You do know how to use this stuff, don't you?"

Dane's attention remained on the woman. "Uh huh."

The clerk nudged Dane's arm, "I asked if you know how to use this stuff. It's mighty important you know what you're doin'."

Dane stared at the clerk. "I heard you the first time. I ain't never used it before but Big John Schmidt is helpin' us and he's used it." He stared again at the woman at the back of the store. "Who is she?"

The clerk grinned, "Guess you ain't met 'em yet."

"Them?"

"Miss Victoria and her sister, Miss Ruby." The clerk leaned in closer to Dane and whispered, "Fine lookin' ladies, the both of 'em. But that Miss Ruby, now she's—well—there just ain't words to describe the lady. She keeps 'em busy at The Tollgate, though. Hear tell she's quite the card player. Miss Victoria bought the store across from the livery and she's settin' up a restaurant and boardin' house."

Dane shook his head as he grappled to understand how this lovely, refined lady could be related to the woman he met at The Tollgate. "You sure they're sisters?"

The clerk nodded. "Yes sir. I heard it from Miss Victoria herself."

The woman approached the counter carrying her purchases. Dane reached out to her. "Here, ma'am, let me take that for you."

She laid her items on the counter.

"Thank you, sir, but I'm quite capable of carrying them myself." She offered a gloved hand. "I don't believe we've met. I'm Victoria Cashman."

Dane wiped his palm on his pant leg and then took the lady's hand in his. "Dane Cholua."

"Cholua?" She tilted her head to one side. "Any relation to Jake Cholua?"

"Yes ma'am. He's my brother."

Her dark eyes sparkled and her lips turned up ever so slightly. "Really?"

"How do you know Jake?"

"Oh, I don't. My sister mentioned meeting him. She seemed quite impressed. Do you live in Black Hawk Pointe?"

"We have a minin' camp up in the mountains."

She paid the clerk for her purchases. "I see." She reached the door and then turned and faced Dane, locking her dark eyes on his and causing his heart to flutter. "I'll be opening my restaurant in a few weeks. Why don't you and your brother stop by for a meal?"

With the fuse wire in hand, Dane hoisted the barrel of black powder onto his shoulder and then joined Victoria. Pushing the door open and holding it back for her to exit he grinned. "We might just do that."

She cast him a sweet smile and then stuffed the mining pan and shovel into her saddlebag. With the grace of an expert horsewoman, she slipped her foot into the stirrup and mounted a large chestnut mare in sidesaddle fashion. And then, after a quick wave of her hand, she rode down the hill toward Black Hawk Pointe. Dane watched until she was out of sight and then loaded his purchases on the pack mule.

He shook his head in wonderment. The woman was refined and spoke like an educated lady. It made perfect sense she would open a restaurant and boarding house—but what was she doing buying a gold pan and shovel?

CHAPTER

That afternoon, Dane and Big John took turns swinging the sledgehammer and Jake held the long chisel against the rock as they formed holes for the powder. They'd made a dozen bores when Big John set down the hammer and grinned. "Think that should do it, fellers. You two go on up while I put in the powder and set the fuses, then I'll come up—and we'll wait for the boom."

Dane and Jake climbed the ladders and then crouched next to the hole and looked down. "You sure he knows what he's doin'?" Jake asked.

Dane bit at his bottom lip. "Yeah—sure—he'll be okay."

John called up, "All set. I just gotta light the fuses."

Moments later, a deafening roar preceded an eruption from below that threw the Cholua brothers a good ten feet back from the opening. The ground where they had been standing caved in and dust and debris shot out. Dane's head pounded, his ears rang and he wheezed and coughed as he crawled through the cloud of dust searching for his brother. "Jake!"

Choking on the thick air, Jake stumbled into Dane and then collapsed on the ground next to him. The older brother grasped the younger one by the shoulders and shook him. "You okay?"

Jake groaned and then sat up. "I think so. Nothin' broken anyway."

They sat for several moments waiting for the air to clear and then Dane knelt gazing in terror at the enormous crater now filled with debris. "Did Big John make it out? Have you seen him?"

Jake looked around and then shook his head. "Ain't seen him or heard him." Tears filled his eyes as he pointed to the cave in. "You think he's alive under there?"

Dane forced back his own tears. "Ain't no way . . . any man could make it through all that."

Jake limped to the tent, grabbed two shovels and then returned to the edge of the debris-filled hole. "Start diggin'. We gotta find him." He began digging and throwing ground. "Come on—Dig. Big John's down there."

Dane's stomach turned, and unbidden tears trickled down his cheeks. He took his brother by the arm and pulled him away from the hole and onto solid ground. He inhaled a deep breath. "Ain't no way we can get to him ifin he's under all that."

Jake squirmed out of his brother's grip and then dropped to his knees. "We gotta try!"

Dane shook his head. "That ground could give way any minute. Big John wouldn't want us killin' ourselves tryin' to get to him and you know it."

He picked up the shovels and walked up to the campsite, leaving Jake shaking with grief at the edge of their dear friend's grave.

Later, Jake joined Dane in the tent and laid on a cot, staring at the ceiling in absolute silence. The sun had set and the locusts began their mournful evening serenade before Dane went outside and stoked the campfire. Jake had slept fitfully letting out an occasional groan and Dane couldn't imagine a nightmare worse than what they experienced earlier that day.

Standing in the firelight with crackling flames warming his face, Dane thought he heard a voice calling. He walked about ten feet away from the campfire in the direction of the sound and listened. Again a call came, this time more clearly.

"Jake? Dane?"

Dane leaned his head to one side and listened. *It can't be. I'm hearin' things.*

Someone called again, "Jake? Dane?"

Now the sound came from the opposite direction and Dane turned to see Big John standing on the other side of the campfire. The whites of his eyes showed bright in the blackness of his face. A broad smile formed on his lips and he grabbed Dane into a tight hug. "Praise God you're alive."

Dane stuttered in disbelief. "John? Is it really you?"

"Course it's me. Who else would it be?"

"But we thought—well when the place caved in—we thought for sure you was . . ."

"Dead? You thought I was dead?"

Dane lowered himself onto a log next to the fire. "How'd you get outta there?"

Jake stood at the opening to the tent, his eyes open wide and arms spread palms up. "What in tarnation? John, is it really you?"

The blacksmith laughed. "I wish you two could see the looks on your faces. I ain't no ghost. It's really me."

Jake grinned and then wrapped his arms as far as he could around the big man. "We thought—well we . . ."

"I gather you thought I was dead." He held his arms wide open. "But as you can see—I'm very much alive." He grabbed up a canteen, gulped down several big swallows and then wiped his mouth with the back of his hand. "Gotta admit I thought I was a gonner when the powder went off as quick as it did. I musta made the fuses a li'l too short. But the blast threw me into one of those tunnels before the whole thing came down."

Dane shook his head. "So how'd you get out?"

"I felt my way along the stream until I found an opening and then I crawled out."

Jake sat on a log across from his brother. "Where does it end?"

"Can't say for sure since I found my way up here in the dark. Saw the glow of the campfire."

"Think you can find it in the daylight?"

Big John nodded. "Probably—yep, pretty sure." He stretched and yawned. "Right now I just wanna sleep. Don't think there's a bone in my body that don't hurt."

The big man disappeared inside the tent as Dane's thoughts returned to the explosion, the cave in and the near deaths of all of them. He raised his eyes to the starlit heavens, "You tryin' to tell us somethin'?"

CHAPTER

The morning sun hung bright in the sky as Dane sipped a cup of coffee while pacing the edge of the campsite. "It's crazy to keep doin' this. We nearly got ourselves killed yesterday."

Big John shook his head. "I don't agree. We've hauled a few hundred dollars worth of gold out of The Hole in the Ground and just cause we had a little mishap ain't no reason to give up."

"Jake and I got enough to get us back home. I'm thinkin' we should quit and do just that."

"You musta took a smack on the head yesterday. You ain't talkin' like yourself. Maybe you just need to rest awhile. Maybe go down to town and have the doc take a look at you. You might have one of them concussion things. I think you shook your brain up in the blast."

Jake appeared from a thicket of trees and then picked up a pick and shovel from next to the tent. "You two gonna sit there all day jawin' or we gonna go find that openin'?"

The blacksmith stood and grinned. "I'm comin' with you." He looked at Dane. "If you ain't comin' along—you may as well go back to town. Me and Jake are gonna find that hole and get back into our claim."

Dane tossed the remains of his coffee into the fire. "You two go on. My head's still poundin' and my ears are still a ringin'."

Big John nodded. "Like I said, it's probably one of them concussion things. You think you can make it to town by yourself."

"Yeah." Dane searched through their boxes of supplies. "Guess we could use some more coffee and a couple other things. I'll take one of the mules down and pick up what we need—and maybe I'll stop by the doc's . . ." He sighed. "And get my head checked out."

Jake and Big John started over the hill. Dane shouted after them. "I still think you're both crazy—just don't get yourselves killed."

Several hours later, Dane loaded the supplies on the back of the mule. The doc had gone up the hill to fix a miner's broken leg. Nobody had any idea when he'd be back. The ringing in Dane's ears had stopped and his head didn't hurt near as bad.

"Well, hello, Mr. Cholua," a female voice called from behind him. "Dane, isn't it?"

He turned to see Ruby and Victoria Cashman strolling along in front of the dry goods store. He tipped his hat, "Mornin' ladies."

Ruby twisted a golden curl between two fingers and winked. "Where's that handsome brother of yours?"

Dane stared at Victoria whose attention seemed directed toward something down the street. "He's up at our claim."

"Your claim?" Ruby's blue eyes sparkled. "You have a mining claim?"

Dane swallowed hard. He hadn't wanted to mention The Hole in the Ground but then just about anyone who wanted to know could go to the recorder's office and find their claim. He gazed into the pretty woman's eyes and for a moment he was as tongue-tied as his brother had been a few nights before. "Yes, ma'am."

He now had Victoria's attention. "And where is your claim, Mr. Cholua?"

Dane pointed toward the mountain. "Up there a ways."

"And do you have a mine or are you panning?"

Dane did not want to share any more information about their claim but Victoria fascinated him. She was so prim and proper—and so pretty. "Panning." He said.

Moreover, it was not a lie. They had not dug out a mine and although they'd followed the stream through the water formed pathways it wasn't technically a mining shaft. "Yeah—panning."

Victoria nodded, her eyes narrowing. "I understand from several of the merchants that you boys have been paying for supplies with some sizeable nuggets. I don't suppose you would be willing to direct me to where I might find my own treasure."

"We done alright, I guess." He stared at the woman's face and then diverted his gaze to the store window behind her. "You plannin' on minin'? Thought you were opening up a restaurant and boardin' house."

Victoria smiled and then covered her mouth with her lace-gloved hand as she chuckled. "Oh, Mr. Cholua, I am a woman of many talents. I'd be happy to share my ideas with you."

Dane looked down at his tattered, dirty shirt and pants and then back at the ladies dressed in their finery. He tipped his hat to Victoria and then to Ruby. It's been mighty nice chattin' with you, but I need to get back up the mountain."

Victoria opened her lace parasol and then rested the handle on her shoulder, shading her upper body. "Maybe next time. I believe I did invite you to stop by my restaurant for a meal. Possibly I could join you and we could chat some more."

Ruby held Dane's upper arm in a soft grip. "And you be sure and tell that brother of yours I have a few things I want to discuss with him as well."

Dane's mind spun and a fluttering took hold in his chest. He had never before met two women so brazen and bold—and yet so beautiful. His gaze fixed on Ruby's deep blue eyes and he inhaled a sharp breath as he stepped back. "I'll be sure and tell him." He then directed his attention to Victoria and tipped his hat. "And I'll take you up on that meal sometime when I'm in town."

Taking hold of the mule's reins, Dane led the animal down Main Street. As he passed The Tollgate Saloon, he glanced up at the open windows occupied by several scantily dressed women. He had never been one to spend his hard-earned money on such pursuits. A lady like Victoria Cashman was more to his liking. A smile formed on his lips as he pondered her dark hair, deep brown eyes, porcelain white skin and trim figure. *Was she plannin' on minin'? She bought a gold pan and shovel. But she bought the vacant buildin' and was openin' a restaurant.* He shook his head and worked to push her from his thoughts.

THE END

Misadventures
of
The Cholua Bros.

Book 2

PISTOLS AND PETTICOATS

BY

MAGGIE MAGOFFIN

CHAPTER

Black Hawk, Colorado
September 1860

T he store clerk lowered his eyes and then shook his head. "Ma'am. It just ain't somethin' ya need to know. I found his body lyin' in the creek up yonder. Why ya wanna go askin' me to tell ya more?"

Victoria Cashman lay her hand on his. "Because I need to know how he died and when."

"Did ya know Mr. Rumson?"

"Yes, I knew him quite well and it is imperative that I know the details of his death." She swallowed past the lump in her throat. "He and I were . . . we were quite close."

The clerk turned his back to her and arranged cans on the shelf. "I'm sorry, ma'am. I understand ya needin' answers, but the plain fact is I can't see how knowin' the gory details of the man's death is goin' to help ya." Turning around, he laid his hands on the counter and faced her. "Just leave it be. He's dead and that's that."

Victoria rolled her eyes and sighed. "Well then, can you tell me who took care of burying him?"

He exhaled and then smiled. "I took him to the undertaker up in Central City. Might be you could talk to him."

Victoria hurried from the general store and up the hill. A week earlier, when she arrived in Black Hawk Pointe, rumors were circulating about Ben Rumson. Some said Indians killed him, scalped him and left what remained of his body in the creek. Some said he passed out drunk in the stream and drowned. Others said someone shot him. She had to know the truth. The man had done more than stolen her money—He stole her heart.

Reaching the livery, she peered in through the open door and called out, "Anyone here?"

A boy with freckles and disheveled blonde hair stepped out of the shadows. "Yes ma'am, can I help ya?"

Startled by his sudden appearance, Victoria inhaled a quick breath. "I need directions to the undertaker in Central City—and I need a horse and buggy."

The boy rested his weight on the handle of a pitchfork, a somber frown crossing his face. "Somebody die?"

"No."

The young man shrugged. "So why you need an undertaker?"

"Someone died but not recently. I was told the undertaker could tell me what I need to know."

"Who was it died?"

His sweet charm and sincere curiosity reached a place in Victoria's heart, causing her to soften her approach and smile. "You ask an awful lot of questions."

"Yes ma'am. Mr. John—He be the blacksmith—well, he told me, 'Timmy. If ya wanna learn anythin' in this life ya gotta ask questions.'"

She laid her hand on his small shoulder. "Did Mr. John also tell you it is not polite to be nosey?"

He hung his head and muttered, "Sorry. Didn't mean to be nosey. The last feller I know died 'round here was that Rumson feller and it didn't seem nobody really cared that he died."

The fact that no one in Black Hawk Pointe cared that Ben was dead pained her, but did not surprise her. He did have a way of rubbing people the wrong way. "Did you know Mr. Rumson?"

Timmy straightened. "Yep, sure 'nough did."

"And you know the details of his death?"

He shrugged. "Ain't no secret. Everybody was talkin' 'bout it."

Yes, everyone had been talking about the murder of Ben Rumson, but who knew the truth of how and when it happened? Rumors and gossip were getting her nowhere. "Can you tell me what you heard, Timmy, and who told you?"

His eyes grew wide and he gave a toothy grin. "Oh, yes ma'am! Mr. John, he done seen the body and I heard him and Mr. Dane talkin' 'bout it. They said somebody done shot him plumb through the back of the head and when that bullet come out of his face it done tore his nose right off."

Victoria's stomach lurched at the thought, but it did make more sense than any other story she heard. Timmy continued with animated gestures, occasionally raising the pitch in his voice, but his chatter was only an echo in her consciousness. The young man's hand gripping her arm brought her back to the present.

"You okay, ma'am?"

She stuttered, "Yes . . . I'm . . . sorry."

"Ya plumb went pale on me there for a minute." He motioned toward a tree stump outside the door. "Maybe you ought to sit a spell."

She inhaled and patted his hand, still gripping her arm. "No. No. I'm fine. Thank you." She forced a smile. "Do you know when Mr. Rumson was killed?"

Timmy tilted his head to one side, scrunching his lips as though deep in thought. "I'm thinkin' they said somethin' 'bout Sam—He be the bartender at the Tollgate—Mr. Dane said somethin' 'bout Sam seein' Mr. Rumson the night before. So I'm guessin' he couldn't a been lyin' in the creek more than a day when they found him." He shrugged. "Just sayin' that's what I figure."

In spite of his tattered clothing and filthy condition, Timmy radiated a youthful, joyous glow. Yet, his eyes held a maturity and sadness Victoria was unable to ignore. She looked around the livery and then back at Timmy. "Do you live here?"

"No ma'am. I live with my ma."

It was a relief to know the boy was not an orphan. "And your pa?"

He shook his head. "Pa was killed in a minin' accident last year. It's just me and ma."

Victoria brought her gloved hand to her chest. "Oh, Timmy, I'm so sorry I asked. It must be painful for you to talk about."

Timmy shrugged. "Oh, it's okay."

"Where do you live?"

Timmy pointed up the hill. "We got us a tent up near Mountain City."

She and her sister, Ruby, had taken a room at Miss Maggie's boarding house until the renovations on the vacant building she bought were completed. She could not imagine living in a tent in this mountain climate, especially during the winter months. Moreover, there was little honest work for women in a mining camp. "What does your ma do while you're here at the livery?"

Timmy chuckled. "You ask an awful lot of questions?"

She laughed. "I am sorry. I'm really not being nosey. It's just that you're such a sweet, well-mannered young man that I'm curious to know more about you."

"Naw, it's okay. I was just joshin' with ya. Ma does laundry and cookin' and whatever else folks will pay her to do. We get by."

Cooking? Victoria had been searching for a cook, but had given up hope, as there were few women in the area and none of the men she met thus far, even if they could cook, were likely to be willing to work for a woman. She pressed her hands together and smiled. "Oh, Timmy, that's wonderful. I'm opening my restaurant in a few weeks and I really need a cook. Could you please ask your ma to stop by Miss Maggie's and talk to me?"

Timmy's nodded his head in a rapid motion. "Oh, yes ma'am. I'm sure she'd like that, and she's a real good cook."

Victoria turned to leave. "Wonderful! I'll look forward to talking to her." She stopped and turned to face Timmy. "By the way, what is your mother's name?"

"Angela, but folks just call her Angie."

"Well, I hope to be able to speak with her soon."

Timmy cleared his throat. "Ma'am, can I ask one more question?"

"Of course, Timmy, what is it?"

He scuffed his worn boot in the dirt, his eyes downcast. "What's your name, ma'am?"

She faced him and laughed a loud guffaw that included an unladylike snort and then put her hands over her mouth. "Oh my, Timmy, I am so sorry. How rude of me. My name is Victoria Cashman." She laid her hands on his shoulders. "You may call me Miss Vicky."

Timmy grinned up at her. "Okay, Miss Vicky. You said you're needin' a buggy and directions to the undertaker. You want I should get that buggy ready for ya?"

She shook her head and sighed. "No, Timmy, I think you've told me everything I need to know."

PISTOLS AND PETTICOATS

Release date: Spring 2015

Maggie Magoffin is a columnist, short story author and novelist with a Bachelors Degree in English and Professional writing.

When she's not entertaining her readers with a novel perspective of the old west, she's most likely traversing the spiraling back roads of her Colorado foothills.

Visit Maggie at www.maggiempublications.com.

www.ingramcontent.com/pod-product-compliance
Lightning Source LLC
Chambersburg PA
CBHW030539180626
46810CB00005B/1941